OUR MAGIC BUNK BED

The Bedtime Adventures of Ally and Arthur

by Adam Zollinger

For my little adventurers

ISBN-13: 978-1491201053
ISBN-10: 1491201053

Hi! My name is Ally,
and I love adventure!

My latest adventure was building a bunk bed with my dad. My dog Hoover fetched all the tools for me, and I tested them out. My little brother Arthur watched, so he could learn how to build stuff too.

What Arthur didn't know was this was much more than an ordinary bunk bed. I had plans to make this bed special and we were going to use it to find the ultimate adventure.

Now, this is probably a good time
to tell you that I know

MAGIC!

Of course, it only works when I put on my
fancy princess dress and use my magic
princess wand; but that is not hard to do.
In fact, I did just that when my dad finished
the bed and had fallen asleep.

I knew that, if I wanted to find the ultimate
adventure, I would have to use my best magic spell
on my new bed. I had to go deep into my spell book
before I found one that was just right. I pointed
my wand at the bed and said,

"One, two, peek-a-boo;
Ally and Arthur say WAHOO!"

Arthur and I had to yell "WAHOO" at the top of our
lungs for the spell to work, and work it did!

POOF!

Instantly the bed transformed into an airplane! Its name was The Sleeping Beauty, and it was probably the fastest plane in the entire world.

I always wanted to be a pilot. The only problem was that I had no idea how to fly a plane - or a bunk bed for that matter. It couldn't be much different than riding a bike, right?

If we were going to have some real fun, I knew we would have to do some tricks. I cranked the wheel hard to the right and performed a perfect barrel roll. "Nothing to it!" I thought. Arthur and Hoover weren't so sure. They felt sick to their stomachs and wouldn't let me do any more tricks after that.

If I couldn't do any more tricks, I knew that flying could never be the ultimate adventure. It was time to search somewhere else. I repeated the spell again,

"One, two, peek-a-boo;
Ally and Arthur say WAHOO!"

BAM!

The bed became a stagecoach and Hoover was our horse. We were in the Wild West.

"This stagecoach is probably full of bags of money," I thought.

I started shouting, "H'YAH, H'YAH," so that Hoover would run faster. I had to keep us safe from any bandits that wanted to steal our precious cargo. After a while, though, Hoover got really tired. I guess he needed some water, but there were no watering holes in sight. Without something to drink, I knew this adventure wasn't going to work out.

At least I looked cool in my pink Cowboy boots. Arthur looked pretty cool in his bandana, too. "Oh well. Let's try this again!" I shouted.

"One, two, peek-a-boo;
Ally and Arthur say WAHOO!"

ZOOOOM!

In a flash we were racing through the desert in a dune buggy. I was the driver, of course, and Arthur was my navigator. Dust was flying everywhere, and we could hardly see. Arthur was screaming from the back, "This road is SOOooOOo bumpy!" I could hardly hear him over the roar of the engine.

I had always thought that a Baja race would be fun, but I began to change my mind just as we ran out of gas. NO FUN!

Apparently, my spell didn't include extra fuel.

Speaking of the spell, it was time to give it another try. This could never be the ultimate adventure if we ran out of gas. Say it with me:

"One, two, peek-a-boo;
Ally and Arthur say Wahoo!"

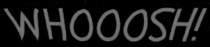
WHOOOSH!

With a rush of wind, the bed transformed again, but this time something was different. Instead of going super-fast, we were going so S...L...O...W....

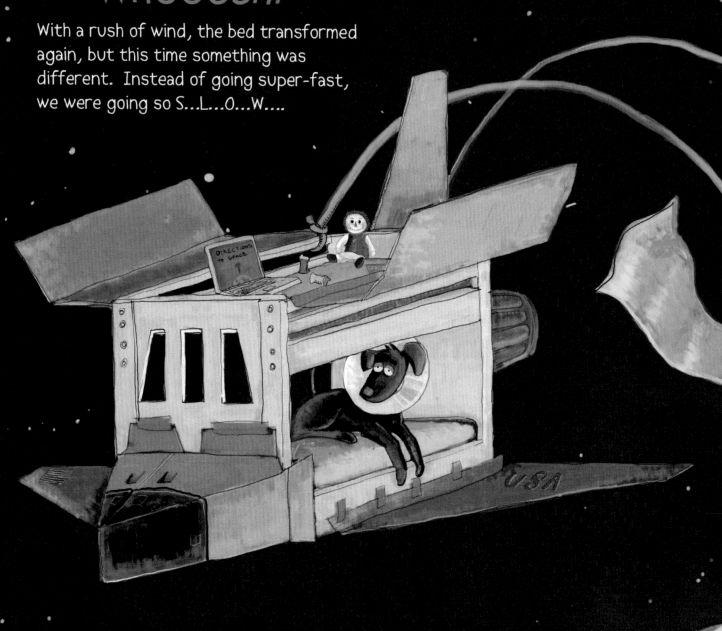

We were astronauts! Arthur and I had always wanted to go to space. It was wildly fun floating through space and practicing my cartwheels without gravity, but eventually we became hungry. We tried some of the space food that I found in our space shuttle, but our fun was over. No great adventure could ever taste that **bad**!

"Time to move on," I told Arthur. "Spell, please!"

"One, two, peek-a-boo;
Ally and Arthur say Wahoo!"

SPLASH!

All of a sudden the bed was floating in the ocean. It was transformed into the Princess of the Sea, the most majestic ship to ever sail the open ocean. Now, sailing the high seas was truly an adventure. I always knew that being the captain of an enchanted ship was the right job for me.

After a while, though, we were lonely out there on the high seas. For as far as the eye could see, there was nothing but dark blue ocean and bright twinkling stars.

"I miss mom and dad," Arthur said.

"I couldn't agree more," I told Arthur. I was ready to go home.

"Woof," barked Hoover in agreement. He wanted to go home too.

"Time for one last spell," I said.

"One, two, peek-a-boo;
Mommy and Daddy, we miss you!"

FLASH!

We were back home. We were all exhausted from our
adventures, but there was still one more place we needed to
go. We gathered our blankies, binkies and sippies, and headed
for mom and dad's room. They were already asleep but we
didn't mind. We nestled ourselves right into their bed. It was
SOOO comfortable.

Now, you have to understand, my dad was no race car driver, and my mom was certainly no airplane pilot. While their bed had no magic powers whatsoever, at that moment, there was no other place in the whole universe we would have rather been.

The adventure hunting would have to wait until tomorrow. Tonight, the ultimate adventure was just being a kid.

GOOdNigHt!

Follow the author at:
http://www.AllyandArthur.blogspot.com
facebook: Our Magic Bunk Bed
twitter: @ourmagicbunkbed

Made in the USA
Middletown, DE
16 December 2017